in the PARK

by Roger Hargreaves

Copyright© 1979, 1982 by Roger Hargreaves
Published in U.S.A. by Price/Stern/Sloan Publishers, Inc.
410 North La Cienega Boulevard, Los Angeles, California 90048
Printed in U.S.A. All Rights Reserved.
ISBN: 0-8431-1103-8

PRICE/STERN/SLOAN
Publishers, Inc., Los Angeles
1983

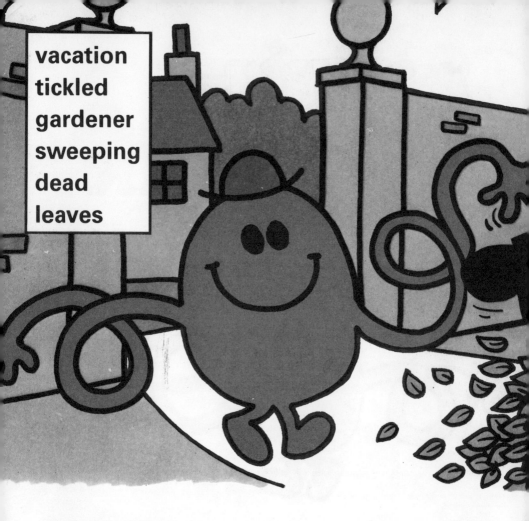

vacation
tickled
gardener
sweeping
dead
leaves

Mr. Tickle was in the park. It was a sunny day, and the children were on vacation from school.

"What a good day for tickling," thought Mr. Tickle.

A gardener was sweeping up some dead

leaves. Mr. Tickle reached out and tickled him. The gardener fell into the pile of leaves.

"It's a good thing you had a soft place to fall," said Mr. Tickle.

edge
group
branch
bounced
appeared
high

At the edge of the park there was a group of trees. Mr. Bounce was walking under a low branch.

Suddenly a long arm appeared from behind a tree and tickled Mr. Bounce, which made him jump! He bounced up to the

4

branch and hit his head. Poor Mr. Bounce!
  But as soon as Mr. Bounce hit the ground
he bounced high into the air again. He
bounced past Mr. Tickle, right to the top of
the tree!

rowboat
middle
stretched
disappeared
oars
pulled

Next, Mr. Tickle went to the lake. Mr. Worry was in a rowboat in the middle of the lake.

Mr. Tickle stretched out his arm and tickled Mr. Worry. Mr. Worry dropped his oars. They disappeared into the lake.

"Oh, dear," said Mr. Worry. "How am I going to get back without any oars?"

Mr. Tickle stretched out his arm again. He pulled the boat to the edge of the lake. Soon Mr. Worry was back on dry land.

crumbs
swans
ducks
pecked
serves
parrots

On the other side of the lake Mr. Wrong
was feeding crumbs to the swans.

"I'm feeding the hens," said Mr. Wrong.

"Those are swans, not hens," said Mr.
Tickle.

Then Mr. Tickle reached out a long arm to tickle one of the ducks. The duck got angry. It pecked Mr. Tickle's finger.

"It serves you right," said Mr. Wrong. "Parrots don't like being tickled!"

clump
sneezing
sticking
among
leaped
reached

Some of Mr. Tickle's friends were playing
hide-and-seek in the woods.

Mr. Sneeze hid in a clump of ferns. But Mr.
Happy heard him sneezing and found him.

Mr. Nosey hid behind a bush. But Mr.

Happy saw his nose sticking out among the leaves.

Mr. Skinny hid in the grass. He lay very still. Then a long arm reached out and tickled him. He leaped up and Mr. Happy saw him.

forgotten
reminded
supposed
explained
throw
greenhouse

In another part of the park, Mr. Tickle
found Mr. Strong and Mr. Forgetful playing
with a bat and ball. Mr. Forgetful had
forgotten what to do with the bat. Mr.
Strong reminded him.

"You are supposed to hit the ball with the

bat," Mr. Strong explained.

Mr. Strong was about to throw the ball when something tickled him. The ball flew out of his hand and hit the greenhouse.

SMASH! went a window. Mr. Tickle ran away as fast as he could!

smelling
flowers
plant
prickly
nobody
believed

Inside the greenhouse Mr. Silly was smelling all the flowers. Then something tickled his head. Mr. Silly looked around. All he could see was a tall plant with prickly leaves.

"It's a tickling plant!" cried Mr. Silly.

He did not see Mr. Tickle hiding behind the plant.

Mr. Silly told everybody that he had been tickled by a tickling plant. But nobody believed him.

bench
faraway
country
fountain
splashing
sound

Later Mr. Tickle found Mr. Daydream sitting on a bench in the rose garden.

Mr. Daydream was daydreaming again. In his dream he was sitting by the sea in a faraway country.

There was a fountain by the bench. It

made a splashing sound. Mr. Daydream
thought this was the sound of the waves in
his dream.

Then something tickled Mr. Daydream. He
stopped daydreaming and looked around.
Who do you think it was?

slide
ladder
hurry
waiting
tightly
bottom

Mr. Nervous was feeling very brave. He quickly climbed up the ladder of the slide. But when he got to the top he was afraid to slide down. Mr. Rush was standing behind him on the ladder.

"Hurry up!" cried Mr. Rush. "I'm waiting."

But Mr. Nervous still held on tightly.

Then a long arm reached up and tickled Mr. Nervous. He let go of the edge and WHOOOSH! The next thing he knew, he was at the bottom of the slide.

picnic
lemonade
tablecloth
upset
cheer
happened

A little later Mr. Tickle found Mr. Fussy and his friends having a picnic. They did not see Mr. Tickle hiding behind a bush.

Mr. Tickle tickled Mr. Clumsy who was drinking lemonade. It spilled all over the

clean white tablecloth.

Mr. Fussy looked a bit upset. So Mr. Tickle
tickled him to cheer him up. What do you
think happened to the cake Mr. Fussy had in
his hand?

tired
thirsty
restaurant
lady
coffee
waitress

By the end of the day Mr. Tickle was very tired and thirsty. He went to a restaurant for a nice cold drink.

But Mr. Tickle could not keep his hands still for long. He tickled an old lady at the next table and made her spill her coffee. He

tickled the waitress and made her drop her tray!

Then it was time to go. When he got home, Mr. Tickle thought about all the people he had tickled that day. There were so many that he was still trying to think of them all when he went to bed!

Questions to talk about

1. What made the gardener fall into the leaves?
2. Why did Mr. Tickle have to rescue Mr. Worry?
3. Who was looking for Mr. Tickle's friends when they were hiding? Did he find them all?
4. Who broke the greenhouse window?
5. Do you think that any plants can tickle?
6. Who was waiting behind Mr. Nervous on the slide?
7. Can you remember all the people Mr. Tickle tickled?